Lindsay
Happy Birthday
Jan. 28, 1999
Love
Grampie &
Meme

Arianna
and the
Strawberry Tea

By Maria Faulconer

Illustrated by
Katy Keck Arnsteen

Ideals Children's Books • Nashville, Tennessee
an imprint of Hambleton-Hill Publishing, Inc.

To my family, with love—M.F.F.

For Mikaela—K.K.A.

Text copyright © 1998 by Maria Fasal Faulconer
Illustrations copyright © 1998 by Hambleton-Hill Publishing, Inc.

Published by Ideals Children's Books
An imprint of Hambleton-Hill Publishing, Inc.
Nashville, Tennessee 37218

Printed and bound in Mexico

Library of Congress Cataloging-in-Publication Data
Faulconer, Maria Fasal.
   Arianna and the strawberry tea / by Maria Fasal Faulconer ;
   illustrated by Katy Keck Arnsteen. — 1st ed.
       p.   cm.
   Summary: When Arianna and her stuffed bear arrive at the elegant
Grand Hotel, where children are not allowed, the looks of horror that greet
them gradually change to appreciation.
  ISBN 1-57102-115-9 (hardcover)
  [1. Hotels, motels, etc.—Fiction.] I. Arnsteen, Katy Keck, ill.
II. Title.
PZ7.F268Ar   1998
[E]—dc21   97-5347
                                    CIP
                                    AC

The illustrations in this book were rendered in
pen and ink, watercolor, and colored pencil.
The text type is in Sabon.
The display type is in Zachary.

First Edition
10 9 8 7 6 5 4 3 2 1

Arianna arrived in a flurry of snowflakes at the Grand Hotel with Monsieur Le Bear and a tattered brown valise. Her parents were detained with the taxi driver, so she marched up the front steps by herself.

For centuries, this elegant hotel had been home to kings and princes, sultans and rajahs, but children and bears—never.

A red-suited doorman guarded the entrance, his nose in the air. Arianna reached up and tugged at his sleeve.

"Excuse me, sir."

He peered down and lifted his eyebrows.

"May we please come in?" Arianna asked.

"Hrrumph," growled the doorman, wrinkling his face.

"Hrrumph to you, too," said Arianna with a smile.

What a funny man! He sounded just like the lion at the zoo.

"We're going to like it here," she whispered to Monsieur Le Bear as they spun through the revolving doors and entered the foyer.

Arianna's boots left snowy puddles on the marble floor as she strolled through the lobby. She was about to step on a thick Persian carpet, when six ladies in white caps raced toward her carrying stiff brooms.

"This carpet looks so soft," Arianna said. "I think I'll squish my toes in it."

So she took off her boots and stepped onto the carpet in her stockinged feet. The parlor maids skidded and fell in a heap at Arianna's feet. Then they stood up and curtsied to her.

Arianna tumbled to the floor, too. Then she jumped up and curtsied back.

"This must be a new dance," said Arianna to Monsieur Le Bear. "We have a lot to learn at this hotel."

Arianna was thirsty after her long trip. She peeked around the corner and saw an enormous room filled with rows of white skirted tables topped with gleaming silver and sparkling crystal. A man in round glasses stood behind a high desk peering into a black book.

"Excuse me, sir," she said, but he didn't notice her. So she walked in and found a small table set for two.

"This will be just right," she whispered to Monsieur Le Bear.

Waiters in black suits whisked by carrying silver trays, but they didn't notice her. She cleared her throat and raised her hand, but they still didn't stop.

"Monsieur Le Bear," said Arianna, "this calls for drastic action."

She unfolded her napkin and threw it on the floor by her chair. The next waiter who passed by skidded to a stop and bent over to pick up the napkin. Arianna leaned forward and met him nose to nose.

"Excuse me, sir," she said.

"And who are you?" the waiter asked.

"I'm Arianna and this is Monsieur Le Bear and we would like a pot of strawberry tea."

The waiter's eyebrows shot up.

"Why, of course, Mademoiselle, strawberry tea. And to eat with that?" he asked.

Arianna consulted with Monsieur Le Bear.

"Two chocolate tarts with whipped cream and a cherry."

Before he could say, "How absurd," two ladies in fur-trimmed suits overheard her request.

"Strawberry tea and chocolate tarts? What a delightful idea! We'll have some, too."

Three rajahs in white turbans overheard the ladies.

"Strawberry tea and chocolate tarts—how quaint! We'll have some, too."

Soon the entire dining room was buzzing with requests for strawberry tea and chocolate tarts.

"You see, Monsieur Le Bear," said Arianna, tucking a napkin under his chin, "I knew we'd feel at home here!"

Meanwhile, the entire kitchen was in a frenzy.
"Get me strawberries! I need strawberries! I must have strawberries!" shouted the chef to the cooks, the stirrers, the measurers, the slicers, the pourers, and all the strawberry scrubbers.

In a flurry of flour, the chef gave orders to whisk the eggs, cream the butter, slice the strawberries, and crimp the crust. Soon, waiters stood ready with trays of tea and tarts for the dining room.

Just then, Arianna's parents burst into the dining room, escorted by the manager.

"Where have you been? We've been so worried," they said. "THIS hotel does not allow children. OUR hotel is across the street."

Arianna gulped. Monsieur Le Bear blinked. Everyone in the dining room gasped.

As her parents prepared to take Arianna and Monsieur Le Bear out of the dining room, the ladies in fur blocked their path.

"No," they said. "This charming young lady has introduced us to a new taste sensation. She cannot leave."

"No," said the manager, as waiters carrying trays of strawberry tea and chocolate tarts flew around the room. "She has increased our business. She cannot leave."

"No," said the parlor maids, joining the
manager. "No one has ever taken off their boots to
walk on our carpet. She cannot leave."

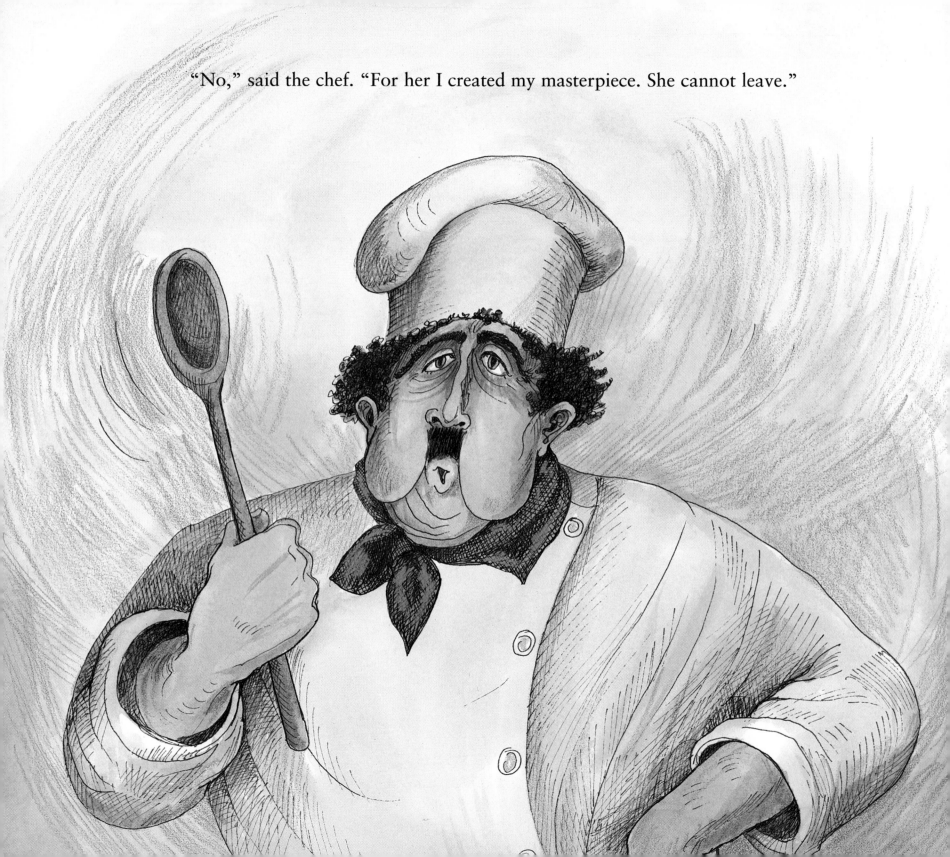

"No," said the doorman. "This is the first time in years that anyone has smiled at me. She cannot leave."

So Arianna and her family were given the presidential suite on the very top floor and all the strawberry tea and chocolate tarts they wanted.

Recipes

Children: Do not make these recipes by yourself. Ask a grown-up to help you.

Strawberry Tea

3 tea bags, orange pekoe or black tea, regular or decaffeinated
2 teaspoons grated orange rind
3 teaspoons strawberry gelatin powder
4 tablespoons honey

4 strawberries, sliced thin (for the pot)
4 cups boiling water
8 additional strawberry slices for garnish
teapot with four cups

In a warmed teapot, place tea bags, orange rind, strawberry gelatin powder, honey, and thin strawberry slices. Pour in boiling water. Stir to combine ingredients. Cover and steep for 3 to 5 minutes. Remove tea bags if desired. Plop 2 strawberry slices in each cup. Top with tea and serve. (Makes 4 cups.)

Chocolate Tarts

Crust:
1 9-inch unbaked pie crust
2 (12-count) mini-muffin pans, ungreased

Filling:
6 ounces milk chocolate chips
1/4 cup half-and-half

Topping:
1/4 pint heavy cream, whipped
1 1/2 tablespoons sugar (optional)

1/8 teaspoon vanilla (optional)
6 maraschino cherries, quartered

To prepare crust:
Preheat oven to 375° F. Place unbaked pie crust on flat surface. Using a 2 1/4-inch round cookie cutter, make circles in the pastry. Press circles gently into the bottom and sides of each muffin cup. Prick bottom and sides of each pastry shell with a fork. Bake in center of oven for 5 minutes. Reduce heat to 350° F and bake for an additional 5 minutes or until a light golden color. Remove from oven. Let cool for 5 minutes before filling with chocolate mixture. Makes approximately 22 tart shells.

To prepare filling and topping:
In medium saucepan, combine chocolate chips and half-and-half. Cook over low heat, stirring constantly until smooth. Remove from heat. With a teaspoon, pour filling into baked tart shells. Refrigerate for at least 30 minutes. When ready to serve, top each tart with a dollop of whipped cream and one quarter of a maraschino cherry. Sugar and vanilla may be added to whipped cream as desired. Makes more than enough filling for 22 tarts.